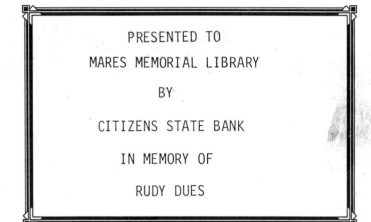
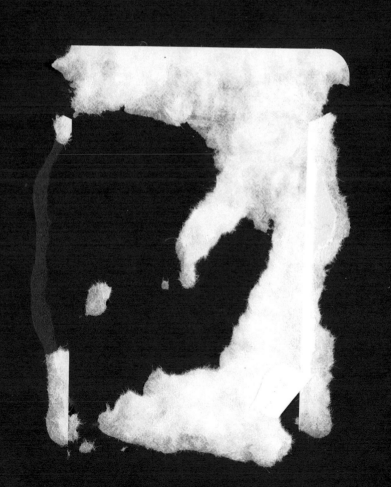

Bounce Back

By Sheryl Swoopes

with Greg Brown
Illustrations by Doug Keith

TAYLOR PUBLISHING
Dallas, Texas

Greg Brown has been involved in sports for thirty years as an athlete and award-winning sportswriter. Brown started his Positively For Kids series after being unable to find sports books for his own children that taught life lessons. He is the co-author of *Mo Vaughn: Follow Your Dreams; Steve Young: Forever Young; Bonnie Blair: A Winning Edge; Cal Ripken: Count Me In; Troy Aikman: Things Change; Kirby Puckett: Be the Best You Can Be;* and *Edgar Martinez: Patience Pays.* Brown regularly speaks at schools and can be reached at pfkgb@aol.com. He lives in Bothell, Washington, with his wife, Stacy, and two children.

Doug Keith provided the illustrations for the best-selling children's book *Things Change* with Troy Aikman, *Count Me In* with Cal Ripken Jr, and *Forever Young* with Steve Young. His illustrations have appeared in national magazines such as *Sports Illustrated for Kids,* greeting cards, and books. Keith can be reached at his Internet address: atozdk@aol.com.

All photos courtesy of Sheryl Swoopes family unless otherwise noted.

Published by Taylor Publishing Company
1550 West Mockingbird Lane
Dallas, Texas 75235

Designed by Steve Willgren

Library of Congress Cataloging-in-Publication Data

Swoopes, Sheryl.
    Bounce Back / by Sheryl Swoopes with Greg Brown ; illustrations by Doug Keith.
        p.   cm.
    Summary: Sheryl Swoopes, member of the Olympic gold medal-winning U.S. women's basketball team, uses her own life as an example of the importance of never giving up.
    ISBN 0-87833-947-7
    1. Swoopes, Sheryl—Juvenile literature. 2. Basketball players—United States—Biography—Juvenile literature.
[1. Swoopes, Sheryl. 2. Basketball players. 3. Afro-Americans—Biography. 4. Women—Biography.] I. Brown, Greg.
II. Keith, Doug, ill. III. Title.
GV884.S88A3   1996
796.323'092—dc20
[B]   96-38712
                                              CIP
                                            AC

Printed in the United States of America

10 9 8 7 6 5 4 3 2 1

My name is Sheryl Swoopes, and I've been playing basketball since I was seven years old.

I've written this book to share with you one great lesson I've learned. It's my experience that no matter how far life pushes you down, no matter how much you hurt, you can always bounce back.

Rich Addicks / Atlanta Journal-Constitution

Basketball has allowed me to experience many wonderful things and has taken me far from my flat hometown roads in Brownfield, Texas.

I know the elation of being a champion. I've felt the pride of playing for my country in the Olympics and winning a gold medal. I've been thrilled by playing a one-on-one game against Michael Jordan. And I've had the satisfaction of being paid to play this game I love.

Laura Wilson

Although basketball has helped me soar high and given me much joy, it has been a tough teacher at times.

The game, just like life, can be rough. Things have happened on and off the court that made me want to quit.

I'm thankful I didn't.

Laura Wilson

Looking back at my childhood in the small town of Brownfield, it's amazing to me how far the bouncing ball has taken me.

Surprisingly, my first dreams had nothing to do with playing sports. If you asked me as a child what I wanted to be when I grew up, I would have said a nurse or flight attendant.

But what I wanted most was to be a cheerleader.

Brownfield, Texas

My first taste of sports came from watching my two older brothers, James and Earl, play basketball.

I remember putting on makeup, dressing like a cheerleader with my cousin, and rooting for my brothers in the gym aisles. We'd also perform at family get-togethers.

Watching the real cheerleaders was great fun. My cousin and I made a promise to each other that we'd both be cheerleaders someday.

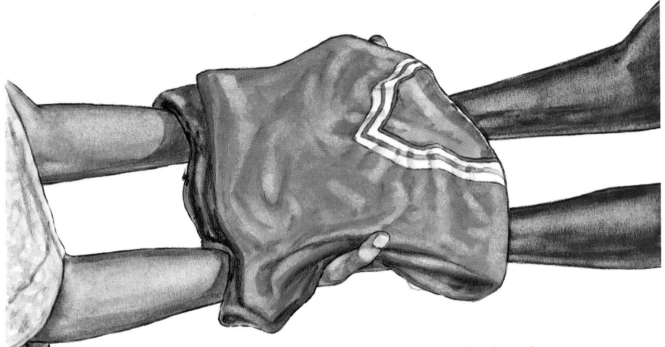

I never kept that promise though.

My father left our family when I was a baby, and I've never met him. My mom, Louise, had to raise James, Earl, myself, and my younger brother Brandon on her own.

Mom did the best she could and sometimes needed public assistance to put food on the table.

I joined the pep squad in sixth grade only because my older cousin had a uniform I could borrow.

I never did try out for cheerleader because I knew we didn't have the money to buy the uniform, pom-poms, and shoes.

Relatives and friends would ask me every year, "Niecy (my nickname taken from my middle name Denise), are you going to try out for cheerleader this year?"

And every year I'd make up an excuse why I wasn't trying out, adding, "Maybe next year."

There were other things I learned to live without.

As I grew older, I said "no thanks" a thousand times when friends asked me to go shopping. Mom bought us a couple new outfits each school year, but some friends bought new clothes every weekend.

That used to bother me. Eventually, I learned not to envy what others had. I understood I had what I had and it wasn't going to change for awhile.

One of the worst things about not having money in high school was never having a car.

Throughout high school I rode the bus to school, and every afternoon I would worry about how I was going to get home. Every day I'd ask a friend if I could bum a ride.

Catching rides might not seem such a big deal to you. It was to me. I never told anyone how much it embarrassed me. I felt like a pest to my friends.

I could hear in my mind what they must have thought: "Gosh, when is Sheryl going to get a car?"

I wondered that myself. I also wondered if we'd ever go on vacation.

When friends said, "Sheryl, where are you going on vacation this year?" My answer became, "Same old thing. Stay in Brownfield and play basketball."

Another dream that never came true was having a perfect family. I'd see friends with their moms and dads at home, going on outings and vacations.

"Why can't that be me?" I asked myself. "Why can't I have a family like that?"

Later I realized that no one has a "perfect" family and what counts most is how you treat the family you have. I didn't have a dad around, but my two older brothers became my male role models.

During my low points I've always tried to turn negatives into positives.

When going without got me down, I'd pump up myself by saying: "It's not always going to be this way. I'm going to make something of myself."

I was determined to keep that promise I made to myself.

I became interested in
basketball at about age
seven. I remember watching
my brothers play basketball in our
driveway and wanting to join the fun.

At first they said, "Basketball is for boys.
You can't play."

It hurt being left out. But I didn't quit asking. I
pleaded, "Please, please, let me play."

Finally, they did. But at first they were cruel. They'd play
keepaway and were rough, hoping I would quit.

They'd knock me down and I'd scrape a knee or elbow. They'd throw me the ball
so hard it'd knock me in the head. I'd run inside crying and tell Mom. At first she
said, "Maybe you should stay inside and play with your dolls."

Every time they pushed me down, though, I'd wipe dry my tears and go back out
to play.

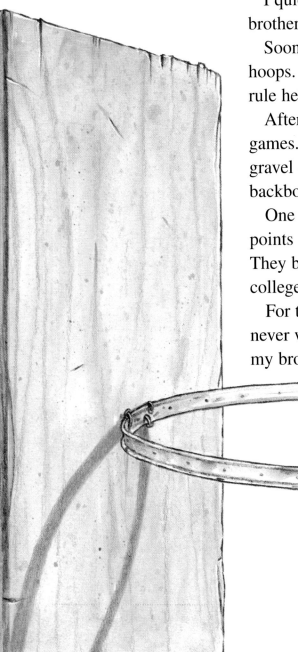

I quickly learned how to dribble and shoot the basketball. My brothers became my best teachers.

Soon I couldn't wait to come home from school and play hoops. But Mom's rule was: Study first, then play. That simple rule helped me keep good grades.

After we'd finished our homework, we'd play our pickup games. We moved around a lot, and I remember playing on a gravel court in our backyard at one house and using a plywood backboard with a rim made from a bicycle wheel at another.

One of our favorite games was "21." The first to score 21 points won. James, 6-foot-4, and Earl, 6-foot-2, could play. They both played high school ball. James went on to play in college.

For thirteen years I had a winless streak against my brothers. I never won a game—until I came home from college. Beating my brothers on our home court ranks as a highlight of my life.

Playing against my brothers prepared me well for organized basketball with girls my own age.

I started playing Little Dribblers at age seven, and it didn't take long for my extra practice to pay off.

From the start, I felt everyone looked to me to be the team leader.

In school, everyone used to call me "Legs." I hated the nickname and sometimes wished my legs weren't so long and that I wasn't one of the tallest in my class.

It's funny how things you get teased about in elementary school can turn out to be your strengths as you grow older.

My long legs certainly help me on the basketball court.

During my third year in Little Dribblers our team qualified for the national championships. Traveling to Beaumont, Texas, for the tournament turned into our family's first vacation.

Our team advanced farther than anyone expected, making it to the title game. Our excitement quickly turned to heartbreak as we lost by a couple points. We all cried.

I felt I let the team down, and it took awhile for me to bounce back. Despite my depression, I kept playing.

I started dreaming about playing high school basketball during junior high. One day during a morning volleyball practice, the high school basketball coach dropped by to watch. We were all nervous because we wanted to impress him with our athletic skills.

"If you keep working hard and doing what the coach tells you, you'll be a very good player," he told me. "And one day you'll play on the varsity team."

That encouraged me to do something every day to improve. Summer time is when I made the biggest gains.

During the summer, I would go to the open gym at the high school three nights a week to play against boys.

"LET HER SHOOT IT."

"HA HA HA!"

"HA HA!"

"HA HA HA!"

"GIVE HER THE BALL!"

"GO AHEAD!"

"HA HA!"

The
first few years I'd
rarely get picked to play, unless
they needed an extra body to fill out a team.
When I did play, the guys never respected my abilities and
rarely passed me the ball. Sometimes at the end of a game, to make fun of
me, a teammate would hand me the ball and shout: "Let her shoot it." Defenders would
step aside to give me an easy layup. Being disrespected like that made me boil inside with
anger. But I swallowed my pride to play because I knew it would make me a stronger player.

Learning skills during those summer nights helped me earn a spot on the high school girls basketball team faster than expected.

After playing in one junior-varsity game as a ninth grader, Coach Dick Faught promoted me to varsity.

I also ran track in high school and even set a school record in the long jump.

One thing I didn't do was run around late at night. Mom gave me a 10 p.m. curfew on weekends.

There were times when I thought her strictness would wreck my life. I now know she did it because she loves me and wanted to keep me out of trouble.

My junior year at Brownfield High our team proved dedication and hard work can take you far.

That year we earned Brownfield High's first girls basketball state championship. We entered the title game as underdogs, with a 29–8 record, against top-ranked Hardin-Jefferson, which was 35–0.

We were down 25–19 at halftime, but we believed we could bounce back.

As one of the taller players in high school, most of my game was taking the ball inside for short-range shots. Against Hardin-Jefferson the inside opened up in the second half and we finally regained the lead with six minutes left. Our upset victory showed all of us the power of teamwork. The magic of winning it all gave everyone in town a special bond of pride.

Sheryl was the only player in double figures and led her team with 26 points and 18 rebounds in the state championship game.

Before my senior basketball season started, my life seemed mapped out because I committed to a college.

One of the top recruits in the state, I accepted a basketball scholarship to play for the state's most successful women's basketball team—the University of Texas Longhorns.

Everyone expected our Brownfield team to repeat as state champions. I soon found out how life doesn't always go as planned.

My final high school game was a bitter loss in district play that knocked us out of the state tournament. I played poorly and once again had a sick feeling inside that I let everyone down—my teammates, coaches, school, and town.

It took some time for me to recover mentally from my disappointment. Later that year, I faced another odd bounce.

Almost the minute I arrived on the University of Texas campus in Austin, I didn't feel right. I went a week before classes and basketball practice started so I could begin to familiarize myself with the school. But it felt too big and too far from home. I flew home that first weekend and decided not to return. I missed Mom, my family, and my boyfriend, Eric Jackson.

I felt terrible about breaking my written promise to the Lady Longhorns.

A lot of people, including a few friends, whispered behind my back that leaving Texas was the biggest mistake of my life.

"Now you'll never win a national championship or be an All-American," people said.

Hearing those comments hurt and motivated me. I wanted to prove they were wrong. I figured if I had the talent and desire to work hard, good things would happen no matter where I played.

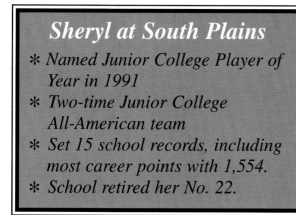

Sheryl at South Plains

* *Named Junior College Player of Year in 1991*
* *Two-time Junior College All-American team*
* *Set 15 school records, including most career points with 1,554.*
* *School retired her No. 22.*

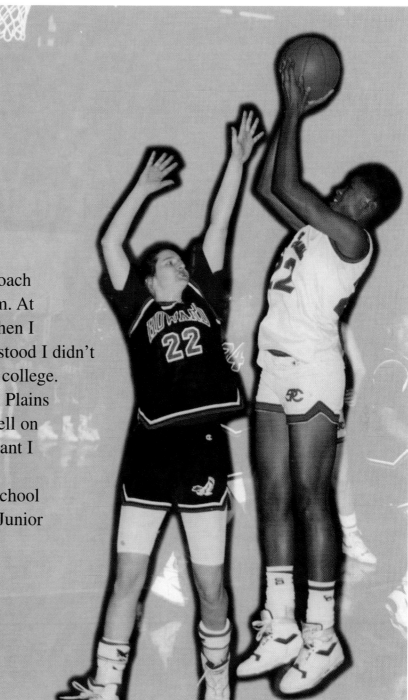

I called nearby South Plains Junior College coach Lyndon Hardin and asked if I could play for him. At first he thought I was playing a joke on him. When I told him I had decided to leave Texas, he understood I didn't want to sit out a year by transferring to a major college.

With Brownfield just thirty miles from South Plains College, my two years as a Lady Texan went well on and off the court. Playing against taller girls meant I needed to improve my outside shot, and I did.

We won 52 games in two seasons and made school history with a sixth place finish at the National Junior College basketball championships.

When it came time to pick another major college, I still wanted to stay close to home. So I chose Texas Tech, in Lubbock, about 38 miles from home.

Playing for the Lady Red Raiders was an exciting next step in my career. Along with larger crowds came increased pressure. My time at South Plains prepared me well, and I fit right in at Texas Tech.

My first season we won the Southwest Conference title for the first time in school history and made it to the NCAA regional semifinals before losing to Stanford, the eventual national champion.

I was honored to learn after the season my name was included in several major college All-American teams. Basketball rolled along just fine until the 1992 Olympic trials.

Sharon M. Steinman

I remember watching the Olympics on television as a kid and dreaming about playing on the USA team.

When I grew up there were no professional women's basketball leagues in America, nothing to look forward to in the U.S. other than the Olympics.

The spring of 1992 I tried out for the Olympic team with confidence and great hope. I made it through the first couple of sessions, but before the final cut I twisted my ankle and wasn't able to finish the tryouts. I didn't make the team.

I returned to Lubbock to complete my spring college courses with a deflated spirit.

A few days later I found myself walking through a Lubbock mall. I enjoy checking out the latest fashion and makeup.

But this day my thoughts were on quitting basketball.

"God, if you love me, why are you letting this happen to me?" I said within myself as I walked. "You know how important the Olympics are to me. Why did you let me get cut?"

At that moment I was ready to give up basketball and find another career and forget about ever playing again.

Then a little seven-year-old girl I never met before walked up to me in the mall and wanted to talk. I stopped, looked down, and smiled as we exchanged greetings.

"I just want to tell you that my mom and I pray for you every night," she said in a sweet, soft tone. "And I just want to let you know God says you're going to be OK, and I don't want you to give up."

In a daze, I thanked her as she walked away. I stood frozen for several minutes and felt chills all over my body. Her simple message jolted me back to thinking positive.

There was much to be positive about as we started the 1992–93 season at Texas Tech. Our team won 12 of its first 15 games and went on to capture its second conference title.

In the conference finals, we faced the University of Texas, the school I left my first week in college. Emotions were high as usual when we played our state rivals. They wanted to prove I made a mistake by leaving. I wanted to prove myself in the playoffs. I think I made my point by scoring a career-high 53 points in the victory.

That put us in the NCAA playoffs a second straight year. This time we kept going and going.

Four more wins put us in the championship game against Ohio State in Atlanta.

Sharon M. Steinman

I felt nervous before the title game. I thought back to losing the big games in Little Dribblers and my senior year in high school and letting everyone down.

Instead of fearing repeated failure, however, I used those thoughts to motivate me.

"OK Sheryl, this is your chance to shine," I said to myself.

I missed my first shot, but didn't let that get me down. I made my next 10 in a row and my teammates kept feeding me the ball, so I kept shooting.

I was in the magical place athletes call "the zone." Everything went in. The basket looked as big as the ocean.

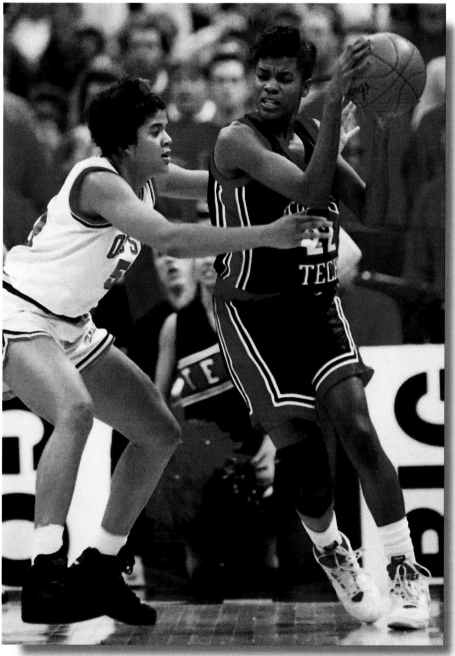

AP/Wide World Photos

Despite my hot hand, Ohio State fought back, and we needed key free throws at the end to hang on for an 84–82 victory and Texas Tech's first national title.

Our celebration erupted when the game buzzer sounded.

I didn't find out my 47 points set an NCAA championship game record until reporters told me afterward. I never thought about individual statistics during the game. All I cared about was winning and showing people they were wrong about me.

After the traditional cutting of the nets, I found Mom and we gave each other a tearful, tight hug.

It seemed like all 150,000 residents of Lubbock greeted our return at the airport. The whole city went crazy for our team. President Bill Clinton even invited us to the White House to congratulate us.

Soon after the hoopla wound down, however, I asked myself, "Now what do I do?"

I discovered quickly things would never be the same.

A few nights later, I ran to the corner store to buy some milk.

People there recognized me and wanted my autograph. Word leaked out and people from all over Lubbock rushed to the store.

Having so many people want my autograph was flattering but tiring. I spent four hours signing autographs.

Soon others wanted my signature on contracts. I tried playing women's professional basketball in Italy, but it didn't work out. I left after ten games because of a contract dispute.

I returned to Texas Tech to finish my degree in general studies and started preparing myself for the 1996 Olympic tryouts, two years away.

Tech coaches gave me specific workouts to improve my speed and strength for international competition. Most of those workouts, though lonely and boring, reminded me that to get anywhere you have to be willing to do something extra every day to improve.

Houston Chronicle

It wasn't all drudgery. Playing any kind of basketball is fun, even pickup games. I played on three U.S. national teams during those years and gained valuable experience. I also helped teach the game at summer basketball camps.

Michael Jordan invited me to work at his camps. One day Michael and I played a one-on-one game to entertain the campers and a TV audience. I had the most fun, though. I scored the first three points before we traded baskets. As we battled, I said: "Just don't dunk on me, OK?"

Michael answered slyly, "I've got to please my campers." Then he went airborne with a Superman jump. I wrapped my arms around his waist and pulled him out of the sky before he could dunk. I surprised both of us. "Oh my gosh, I just fouled Michael Jordan!" I thought.

Michael's competitiveness kicked in and he won 7–5, ending it with a high-flying jam.

Nike, the shoe company, gave me another link with Michael Jordan when in 1995 they offered to create a basketball shoe with my name, called the Air Swoopes.

I felt honored Nike picked me, but my attitude all along has been that I'm glad someone finally made a shoe for women.

The past few years I've worked with many famous people—Kareem Abdul-Jabbar, Spike Lee, and various TV personalities. It's been exciting to meet them, but the person I want to spend most of my free time with is still Eric Jackson.

Because he felt the same way, we were married in June of 1995.

That same month the tryouts for the 1996 women's Olympic basketball team started.

The week-long tryouts were the toughest I ever experienced.

There were twenty-seven women competing for twelve spots. It was intense and nerve-wracking.

We practiced for three months before beginning our 52-game schedule that took us all over the country and to four continents—a trip totaling 102,000 miles.

In our fourth game, we were all reminded how we were more than a team—we were ambassadors for our sport.

We visited a hospital in Virginia and met a frail sixteen-year-old girl dying of leukemia. Her last wish was to watch us play the next night.

The next day, however, word came that the girl had died that morning at the hospital, her simple wish unfulfilled.

With heavy hearts we said a prayer for her. Knowing what we meant to her inspired us and helped us realize we carried to Atlanta the hopes and dreams of many young girls.

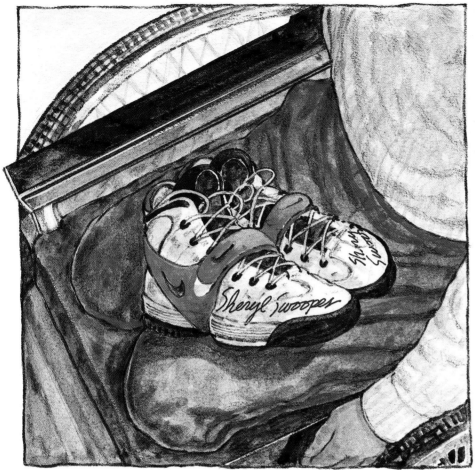

Before the game, I ran to him at courtside and gave him a pair of my Air Swoopes shoes and autographed them. His face lit up the gym.

"I don't know what I'll do with these, I can't wear them," he said.

"You can put them on your wall or some-thing, but I'd love for you to have them," I answered.

Tears rolled down the ex-soldier's face and his joy radiated warmth.

Experiences like those made touring enjoyable.

Still, hectic traveling drained me physically and mentally. I'd wake up and not remember what city I was visiting.

One morning I ordered room service and waited three hours. I called back and discovered I had given my room number from days ago.

My husband traveled with me at times, and he gave me encouragement when I needed it.

Another touching moment came a month later when we played at Vanderbilt University.

I learned that a special Vanderbilt fan wanted to meet me—a Vietnam veteran whose war wounds left him without legs below his knees. He had seen me play when our Texas Tech team knocked out his team in the NCAA tournament.

I had a few rough days when out of exhaustion I told Eric, "I can't do this anymore. I can't go another day."

"Are you going to give up everything you dreamed about because of a few bad days?" he said. His strength empowered me to keep my Olympic dreams alive all the way to Atlanta.

Allsport

Finally, July 19, 1996, marked the 100th opening of the Summer Olympics.

Walking into the packed stadium with the world watching gave me a fantastic feeling of unity and excitement.

We sailed through our competition and into the gold medal game as we hoped.

We stayed in a hotel across the street from Centennial Park. The men's Dream Team was in the same hotel, so we hung out with them and watched their games.

Half way through the

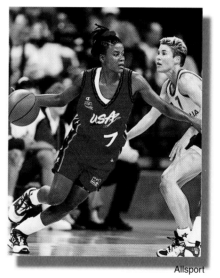

Allsport

Olympics a terrible act put the Games in doubt—a pipe bomb exploded in Centennial Park.

A few minutes before the blast I was going to the same park to check out the concert. But I stopped in the hotel's main floor to talk with teammates.

My husband rushed downstairs and told us about the bomb that killed one and injured hundreds. We were shocked, confused, and frightened. But once officials decided to continue the games the next day, we knew we had to finish our mission.

Playing Brazil in the gold medal game was ironic. Brazil had beaten our USA team by three points in the semifinals of the 1994 World Championships, and we had to share a humiliating bus ride with the victors.

In Atlanta, we both won seven straight to make the title game. So to be the best we had to beat the best.

My defensive assignment was to cover Brazil's best shooter. I wanted to play her tough early to set the tone. But a few minutes into the game, I quickly picked up two fouls. Coach Tara VanDerveer's rule was if you committed two fouls in the first half you'd sit out until halftime, so I knew I'd be benched when I heard the whistle.

I sat at the end of the bench and thought I'd blown the biggest game of my life. Coach called me to her side and calmed me down. She said if I played smart she'd put me back in. I went back on the court and made the most of my second chance.

We beat Brazil convincingly with defense and our inside game. Everyone on our team played and scored, a perfect ending for our long journey together.

Sheryl's Scoring

Team score	Pts
USA 101, Cuba 84	12
USA 98, Ukraine 65	11
USA 107, Zaire 47	11
USA 96, Australia 79	17
USA 105, Korea 64	12
USA 108, Japan 93	9
USA 93, Australia 71	16
USA 111, Brazil 87	16

Allsport

As the final seconds ticked away, the realization of our dreams unleashed a burst of emotions. We screamed. We hugged. We cried. We danced as music blared: *Cel-e-brate good times, come on!*

Some even did cartwheels on the court.

Those moments will always be treasured in my heart along with what a stranger said to me moments after the game. This man congratulated me and said: "I just watched great basketball."

He didn't say great women's basketball. He said great basketball. And that's exactly what we wanted to show the world—that we can play.

Winning the hearts of fans was just as important as winning.

We all gathered one last time on the victory stand to receive our gold medals. The fourteen months of sacrificing, living out of a suitcase, and practicing countless grueling days finally paid off.

Tears of pride streamed down our faces as we accepted our medals for ourselves, our families, our country, and our sport.

I slept with that gold medal under my pillow the first night before putting it in a safe deposit box.

When I hold it now, I still don't believe it belongs to me, the little girl who grew up in West Texas.

Time will tell if our incredible 60–0 run will help women's basketball grow. I hope to play my part in the sport for many years.

I know the future holds good days and bad days. I hope my life shows that dreams can come true. No matter what adversity you face, if you strive to improve every day and set high goals, you will always bounce back.